AUTHOR'S NOTE

Gold leafing is an art form invented by the Egyptians three
millennia ago. To make gold leaf, gold is pounded into thin sheets
that are then layered between paper and pounded some more.
Finally, those gold sheets—now as thin as butterfly wings—are pressed
against an object's surface and applied by brush. Many buildings
and decorative items have gold-leaf details. The effect of gold
leaf on an object is long-lasting and luminous.

Kirsten Hall is the author of *The Jacket*, a *New York Times*
Notable Book of 2014. Her grandfather was responsible
for the gold leafing of many famous gilded buildings in NYC,
including Lincoln Center, Rockefeller Center, Carnegie
Hall, and the Helmsley building.

Matt Forsythe lives in Montreal where he makes picture
books and comics and designs for animation. His first comic,
Ojingogo, was nominated for an Eisner Award. He was also
lead designer on the animated TV show, *Adventure Time*.

The Gold Leaf

For Moredaddy
—K.H.

For Eden
—M.F.

www.enchantedlionbooks.com

First edition published in 2017 by Enchanted Lion Books,
67 West Street, Unit 317A, Brooklyn, New York 11222

Text copyright © 2017 by Kirsten Hall
Illustration copyright © 2017 by Matthew Forsythe
Edition copyright © 2017 by Enchanted Lion Books
Book design: Jonathan Yamakami

A CIP record is on file with the Library of Congress

ISBN: 978-1-59270-214-5

Printed in China by RR Donnelley Asia Printing Solutions
First Printing

The Gold Leaf

Kirsten Hall
Matthew Forsythe

ENCHANTED LION BOOKS

NEW YORK

In spring, the leaves returned.

Soon there was green everywhere.

Jungle green, laurel green, moss green, mint green,

pine green, avocado green, and, of course, sap green.

Meanwhile, a squirrel crept from its burrow, nose twitching.
A chiffchaff called, *chiff chaff, chiff chaff!*
A traveling toad set out in search of a suitable pond.
And the first bluebell blossomed deep within the woods.

Amid all of the newness and excitement, no one caught sight of something most unusual. Something that shone and sparkled.

A gold leaf!

Each wanted it more than anything else in the world.

But who would get it first?

A bird, of course! A warbler swooped in and plucked the leaf from its branch. Oh, how it would brighten her nest!

But when she dove down to show off her prize to the others,
a chipmunk snatched it and ran away.

The leaf would look much better in *his* burrow, he decided.
But then...

A mouse pounced on the leaf and made a great escape.
A golden blanket of his very own!

He scampered home to hide his treasure.
But before he could even get there...

A deer stole the leaf right from his little mouth.

She nibbled its edges. Even its taste was perfect.

Finally, a fox seized the leaf.

Because if everyone else wanted it, well then, he did too.

But then the fox saw that he didn't really have the gold leaf after all.

Tattered and torn, it lay in pieces at the animals' feet.

The forest grew still. The only sound was the wind rustling the leaves, which sent bits of gold swirling in every direction.

With sorrow, the animals realized that their precious leaf
was gone.

The days of summer were long and bright.
The animals were so busy that they slowly
began to forget about their gold leaf.

Autumn arrived, with its brilliantly-colored leaves and many yellows—waxberry yellow, bumblebee yellow, mustard yellow,

candle-glow yellow, maize yellow, harvest-moon yellow,
even yellow ochre. But none were gold.

Winter brought bare branches and short days.

The animals huddled and cuddled. Some even went off
to hibernate and fell into a deep sleep.

And then spring arrived once more.
The leaves that had been forming
burst from their branches.
Soon there was green everywhere.

Pear green, pickle green, parakeet green, juniper green,

crocodile green, lime green, and, of course, sap green.

Meanwhile, a warbler sat tall and alert in her nest.
A chipmunk crept from his burrow, eyes wide.
A mouse came out from his hole into the sunlight.

A deer stopped in her tracks.
And a fox crawled out from under a bramble, ears pricked.

A gentle breeze blew.

Something shone and sparkled.

The forest was alive with wonder.

But this time, no one wanted the gold leaf.

Their happiness was that it had come back to them after all.

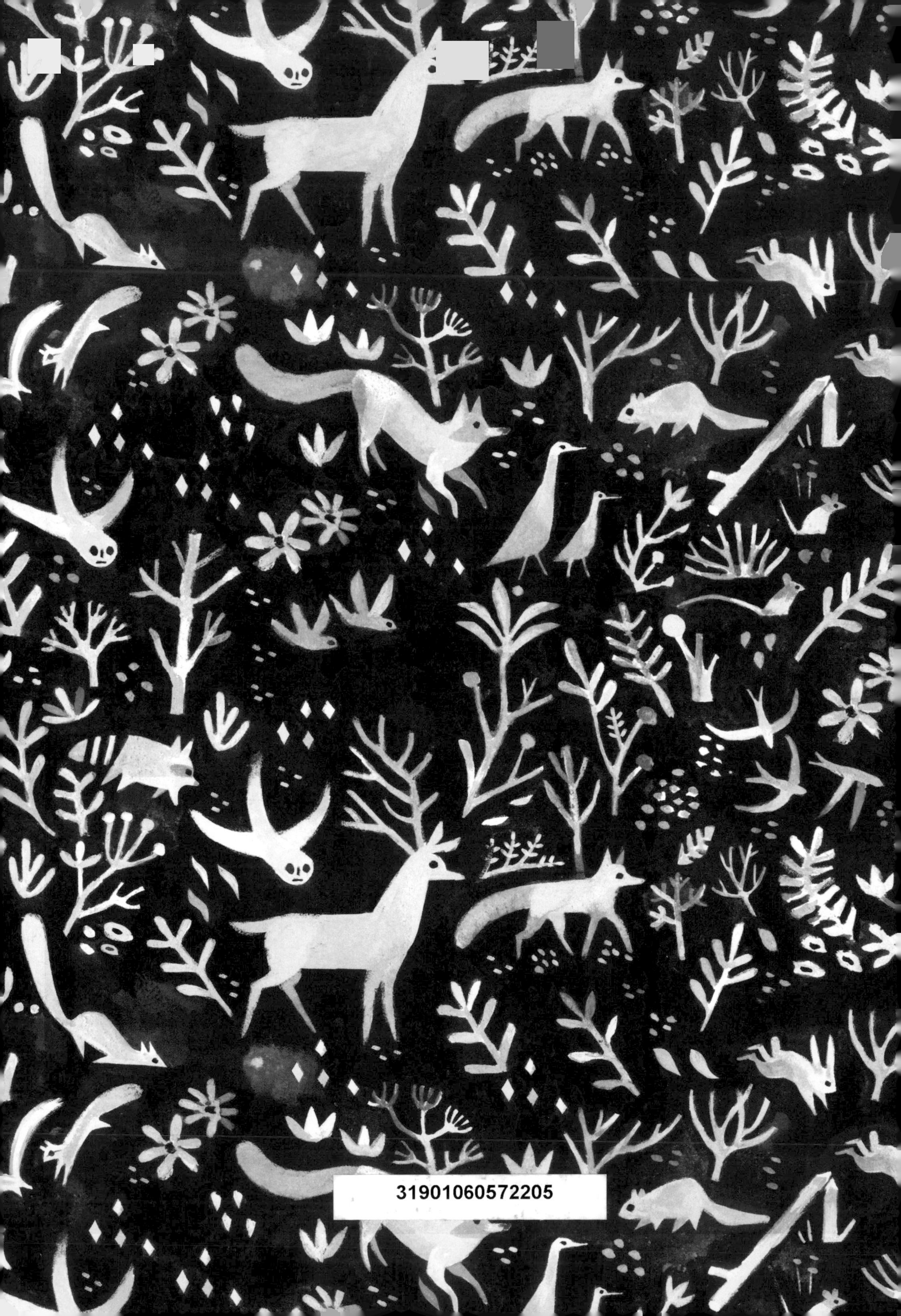